CHRISTMAS

in

Heaven

Susan Elizabeth McMahan

LifeRich Publishing is a registered trademark of
The Reader's Digest Association, Inc.

LifeRich Publishing books may be ordered
through booksellers or by contacting:

LifeRich Publishing
1663 Liberty Drive
Bloomington, IN 47403
www.liferichpublishing.com
844-686-9607

ISBN: 978-1-4897-3661-1 (sc)
ISBN: 978-1-4897-3660-4 (e)

Library of Congress Control Number: 2021912583

Print information available on the last page.

LifeRich Publishing rev. date: 08/04/2021

This book is dedicated to my big brother in Heaven. I can't wait to hear your voice and hug you for the first time.

Contents

Chapter 1

THE WAY IT USED TO BE

I remember the excitement of Christmas as a child. I always looked forward to waking up early and running into the living room to see what gifts Santa Claus had left under the tree. Of course, it was always a race between my brother, my sister, and me. We wanted to see who would be the first to wake up and then wake Mom and Dad. We would bounce on their bed like a bunch of wild monkeys, tugging and pulling on their covers. "Wake up, Daddy! Wake up, Mommy! Santa Claus has been here! He left presents!" we would shout.

Poor Momma and Daddy would moan, groan, and reluctantly roll out of bed to put their slippers and robes on before heading to the living room with us.

"I just need to brush my teeth," Momma would say.

"I'm gonna get some coffee started," Daddy would grumble.

"Oh no," we would moan.

Donald, my brother, and I would follow Daddy into the

kitchen and jump up and down, waiting for what seemed like forever for him to get the coffee pot started. (You know, they didn't have Keurig machines back in 1981.)

My little sister, Noel, would follow Momma into the bathroom and play with her makeup brush while bouncing up and down, waiting for Momma to brush her teeth. Momma would then wash the sleep out of her eyes, comb her hair, and put a little lip gloss on before heading out to where Daddy was lurking with his home movie camera. And she usually gave Noel a little lip gloss for being so patient while she waited for Momma to get ready.

Soon, Daddy would have out his movie camera, coffee would be ready, and we would all be begging to tear into our presents. Donald always wanted to go first. He and I would argue until Momma and Daddy reminded us that the youngest usually goes first. We would impatiently agree to watch Noel, and then Daddy would tell Donald and me to race to see who could open our presents first. Of course, then we'd show one another the goodies that Santa had brought us.

We each got to pick out a gift for our siblings too. I remember how Donald and I would find the funniest gifts for each other. He gave me a sock puppet he'd made one year. I gave him a pet rock another year. But I remember there was the one year that Donnie, as I called my older brother, got me one of my most favorite gifts! I had just given him a mixed tape of recorded music. We laughed because it was primarily made of songs that only I listened to back then. Then I opened my box, totally expecting another usual funny from him, and instead, I found the cutest little birthstone ring. I really had never had a ring, so

I was thrilled. He'd saved his money from mowing lawns over the summer and bought Noel and me two nice gifts. Mom and Dad were super proud of his little hint of maturity that year.

I remember Momma's breakfast that would follow the gifts. I can still smell the homemade biscuits and gravy. And we always had a jar of Nana's grape jelly on hand. I can still remember the taste of that sweet, delicious spread over those warm buttered biscuits. Man! Those were some good times.

Too bad the memories of Christmas weren't always happy. There came a time when all of that was so distant a memory that I didn't even know if I could remember it anymore. It was like all those good things were completely overshadowed by the one thing I could not forget. Losing Donald was all it took. Life would never be the same for any of us again. Christmas would never be the same.

Thankfully, God had not given up on me.

Chapter 2

THE NEWS

I'll never forget sitting in my college class the day I got the news. I was in the middle of an English literature exam. As I took my time to work and ensure that I answered every question to the best of my ability, it didn't occur to me that I was one of the only ones left in the room, taking my test. Most of the class had finished and were long gone. Before I knew it, I was the last student there. It was almost as if I sensed that something big was happening and didn't want to face it.

I went up to the desk to turn in my test, and my professor stopped me. "Lizbeth, there's something I need to tell you. Could you have a seat?"

"Sure." I turned around and sat at a desk, knowing that this was odd.

"I'm terribly sorry, dear. Your mother wants you to call her right away. Something is wrong, and they cannot find your brother."

Why in the world did my English lit professor know all

of this? Why was she telling me this? I knew in my heart that something was wrong. Something was bad.

"Okay, yes … of course," I finally replied after what felt like an eternity.

"She said for you to call her at home. There's a phone in the office around the corner if you need to use it, dear."

"Uh, no. No, that's not necessary. I have my cell phone here. I can just use it. Thanks."

I began to dial and noticed that my professor was staying nearby as if she, too, could sense that this was not good. Normally, that would bother me as I got on the phone. But for whatever reason, I appreciated the comfort at this time. Her concern and care were what I needed before I even knew it.

"Mom, it's me, Lizbeth," I said when my mother answered the phone. "Is everything all right?"

The next few minutes are kind of a blur now, honestly. My memory of what she said is so, so clear, yet so … foggy. And still, it's a memory that is seared into my brain. Donald was missing. He hadn't come home from school on Friday. Mom felt sure he'd been somewhere with his friend Devin, but Devin hadn't heard from him either. I could hear the sheer panic and terror in her voice. She was worried, angry, terrified, and heartbroken all at once. Hearing that kind of fear in my mother's voice was gut-wrenching—especially knowing what I know now.

Chapter 3

AN ACCIDENT

We later learned why Donald had never made it home. They found his car crashed off an embankment on one of the back roads not far from the fast-food place where he worked part time. It was determined that he had been trying to use his cell phone while driving and ran off the road. He hit a tree. A stupid tree.

My mother and father were never the same again. None of us were, really. At least once or twice a week, Mom would go in her room and shut the door after dinner. I could hear her sobbing. I'm pretty sure that evenings were hardest for her. At work, she could stay busy and be distracted by other people and other things. When she was home, however, she was surrounded by memories. His clothes, his photos, his trophies, his room—it was as if you could just smell his cologne by being in the house. He had gotten a small bottle of it for Christmas from Noel and me, but he never wore it or seemed interested in it until he rushed to work one day after football practice. Donnie, as Noel and I called him, thought his quick shower and a couple of sprays of cologne would mask the fact that he had forgotten to wash his work uniform. A girl he worked with told him he smelled good, and he must've like that because he wore it every day after that. Now, even with him gone, it was as if it just drifted through the hallways and up the staircase of our house.

Dad would go to the den and turn on his evening shows. He would watch and then fall asleep. There wasn't a football game he'd miss, though—I guess because Donnie loved football. He wouldn't really talk about anything much anymore. He seemed so sad, still, and lost.

Noel and I had a hard time too. She slept in his T-shirts, and she took a pillow from his room to cuddle up with at night. It helped her because when we were smaller, she wouldn't go to Mom and Dad's room when she had nightmares. Instead, she'd come pile up in a bed with Donnie or me. Donnie was always a little more patient with her than I was. His little sister could do no wrong.

I remember being angry at my brother. We'd always had a love-hate relationship but were fairly close as teenagers. We'd cover for one another when we feared we'd be in trouble. We would share study tips or secrets about mutual teachers and friends in school. He rode to school with me for two years when I got my license. I let him practice driving in my car. He was a prankster. Donnie would do things just to get a rise out of me and out of the whole family. One time, he put a rubber tarantula in my bed between the sheets. It popped up when I pulled the covers back, making it seem as if it jumped out at me! I remember screaming so loudly the whole house came to see what was wrong. I got so mad at him that I glued the pages of his homework together. We would fight and pester each other all the time. We could give each other heck, but nobody else better mess with either one of us. That's just how it was, and it was also why I was so upset with him.

I remember sitting in his room one day and asking, "Why did you take that road? What were you doing on your phone?"

I would shout at his pictures, "You know better!" But it didn't do any good. I couldn't hear his voice anymore. I wouldn't hear his voice anymore. He wasn't going to talk back. It wasn't doing me any good, but I was still angry.

We still had things to do together. Who was going to shoot hoops with me at midnight? Who would I go to when I needed to get an honest opinion about a guy I wanted to date? Why the hell did he have the phone in his hand? He knew better! I was angry at God and angry at Donnie.

Chapter 4

CHRISTMAS EVE

I don't know how or why, but after being seemingly overcome by grief, my mom somehow worked through her heartache. She was able to forgive God. She wasn't angry anymore. I know that sounds incredibly noble, but it made me even more upset. How could she love God and continue to claim His promises when He took her child from her? God didn't protect Donnie even though he was a Christian. Our family wasn't perfect, but we sure weren't living in the amount of sin that other people were.

Mom wanted me to go to church with her, but I couldn't do it. I couldn't set foot in that building knowing that God had ripped my family apart. I couldn't sit in a pew and act like everything was okay. I wasn't going to pretend that I wasn't mad about losing my brother. Yet, it didn't stop Mom from asking me to come. Every time there was a special event or a holiday, she would ask. I hoped that she'd give up or forget, but she didn't. I would use every good excuse in the book. "I have to work. I need to clean house and wash clothes. I have a headache." You name it, I tried it—all because I just wasn't ready to face God or to pretend I liked Him, especially after He jerked the rug out from under us and broke our hearts forever.

Mom asked me to join her and Dad for the Christmas Eve candlelight service. I didn't want to go, but I was tired of hearing her ask. And, quite frankly, I felt guilty about the idea of not going for her at Christmas. This time of year was especially difficult. She wanted everything to be perfect, and she tried so terribly hard to make things as nice as she could for all of us, despite that there was someone missing. So, being the best daughter I could, I told her I would go. I wasn't exactly sure what that meant; I just knew that I would go at the last minute, get my seat in time for the service to start, count the minutes until it was over, and then give hugs and head out as quickly as possible. It was going to be a gift for my mom, and that's all that mattered. She would be happy. That's what was important to me.

When Christmas Eve came, I spent the afternoon wrapping last minute gifts. I also made a dessert to take to Mom's house the next day for lunch. We stopped having breakfasts on Christmas Day. No one ever really mentioned why, but I am pretty sure that we all avoided it because of the empty chair at our table. Even years after the accident, even with additional family members and guests, that chair was never filled again. It somehow became a great place for coats, bags, and other items. Donnie would probably laugh about it, honestly. He used to say that his seat had his name on it, and no snotty-nosed girls were going to plop their tails into his seat. It was meant for strong, muscle-bound men like him. Ha! I laughed at the idea because Donnie was strong, but he was not exactly the Incredible Hulk. Anyway, he got his wish. No one else was in his seat, especially not any snot-nosed girls.

I had been watching a Hallmark Christmas movie to pass the time, stalling until I absolutely had to get ready. I put on my green sweater, brushed my hair, and put on some lip gloss. I took a deep breath, put on my coat, grabbed my purse and keys, and headed out the door. On the way over, I started getting frustrated. "Why did I agree to this?" I asked myself. "What was I thinking?" I didn't want anything to do with church or God. I didn't want to be there, period.

As I sat at a red light on the way, "Mele Kalikimaka" started playing on the radio.

"Is this a joke?" I thought to myself.

Donnie loved that song and would act like such a dork, hula dancing around to it. Here I was, trying to be mad over him, and *that* stupid song came on! I was so mad, but then I burst out laughing. The laughter turned quickly to tears, and I began to sob.

"Dang it, Donnie!" I said aloud. I wanted to curse.

Then suddenly, a honking horn blared. The blurry red light had changed to green. I had no idea how long I had been sitting there, but it had been long enough to tick off the person behind me. I wiped my eyes and pulled around the block to the church. As I put the car in park, I grabbed a tissue out of the console, patted my eyes, and wiped my nose. I took a deep breath and one last glance in the mirror and then headed inside to meet my mom and dad.

Chapter 5

GETTING IT OVER WITH

The service started at 6:00 p.m., and I had timed it just right. I slid in the pew next to Mom and Dad at 5:59 p.m.

"Hey, love! You made it. Is everything all right?" Mom asked.

"Yes, of course," I lied. "I just got caught up in watching a Christmas movie."

The music began to play. Thank goodness! I was going to get this over with. While I was sitting there feeling sorry for myself, the choir began to sing "Joy to the World." It was beautiful, I have to admit. It's hard to continue one's own pity party when thinking of the birth of the savior of the world. But still, I had every right and reason to be angry with Him. God made the choice to send His own son to die on this earth. That was His choice—but I didn't have a choice. My mom and dad didn't have a choice! What gave Him the right to just take Donnie and tear our happy family apart?

When the preacher got up to speak, I realized I had tuned out at some point. Okay, well, I tuned out at a couple of points. I was just taking up space and occasionally would nod and smile at Mom and Dad to appease them. Then I heard Pastor Chuck say these words: "Christmas is not always a time for joy for everyone."

"I'm sorry. What did he just say?" I wondered to myself.

"Many of us think of Christmas, and our hearts break. It's hard for us because there's someone missing at the table now. Or maybe we can't celebrate together anymore because our family has become broken," he continued.

"Yeah. I'm listening," I thought. "Tell me something I don't know."

"It's true. Nothing can make that pain go away. No one can fix us but Jesus."

"Then why hasn't He fixed me?" I could feel myself smirking.

"Just look around this room. Every person, every face is somebody with a story. Every story has a heart, and we never know the love or the heartache that someone may be facing."

I began to look around at the other faces in the room. Admittedly, I hadn't thought about anyone else going through what our family had gone through. I was just hurting. But as I looked around the sanctuary, I noticed a little girl in a wheelchair to the front right. I wondered how long she'd been in a wheelchair. She couldn't be more than thirteen years old. I saw an old friend from elementary school whom I hadn't seen in years, sitting with her mother. I remembered she'd just lost her dad to cancer this past summer. I don't know that I even attended the funeral or sent her a card.

There was an older man sitting by himself in the back. He seemed lonely. I don't know why I felt that way. I certainly didn't know him personally. He just had that look about him. Then there was a young couple sitting in front of us. I don't know what had happened to them, but she was visibly wiping tears from her eyes with tissue. Clearly, something the preacher said had triggered the waterworks. Her husband had his arm around her, and even he had tears in his eyes. There were several other people in the room, and something about all these people caught my attention. I'm not sure why. Maybe they were putting off the same negative energy that I was. Maybe it took a hurt to know a hurt.

"One thing we can count on: there will be a day when the hurt will be no more. The pain we once knew on this earth will all be washed away," the preacher continued.

"Yeah, yeah, yeah. I've heard it all before," I repeated to myself. I was the epitome of cynicism. I knew the spiel. Everything was peachy in Heaven. That still didn't make me any less angry at the time.

Then Pastor Chuck said, "Brother Russ is gonna come up and play a song for us at this time."

I didn't know who Brother Russ was, and I didn't care. "How much longer is this going to last?" I wondered as I looked at my watch.

"Now, this is not a typical Christmas song. I know it's not even a Christian song if you wanna get right down to it. But when Pastor Chuck asked me to sing tonight, I couldn't shake the feeling that somebody here might need to hear this song tonight. So, if I'm wrong, forgive me. I just pray the Lord will use it to speak to your heart, if you're truly missin' someone special in your life this Christmas," Brother Russ explained.

He was a small man, neatly dressed in a button-up shirt and blue jeans. Clearly, he was as country as cornbread, based on his cowboy boots, belt buckle, and southern drawl. He was fairly handsome and soft spoken, and he held a guitar as he stood near the mic. He was basically a Brad Paisley look-alike. He started to play the song "If Heaven Wasn't So Far Away." My first thought was, "Is this a joke? Am I getting punked? Does God have a sick sense of humor or what?" As I listened to the words, I found myself confused. Why would he play a song like this at Christmas? Wasn't this supposed to be a Christmas Eve service? I wanted to get out of there and quick.

Tears began to well up in my own eyes. Everything got blurry. "Don't cry. Don't cry. Stay strong. Pull yourself together, Lizbeth," I told myself. The song talked about visiting Heaven and seeing loved ones who had passed. I mean, really? What were the odds? It was crazy how that song just had to be playing the night I came to church.

Finally, the song was over. The children's choir sang next. Some church members shared scripture. The preacher spoke once more; and this time, he shared about the gift of Jesus. He told us how just as His birth came unexpectedly and in an unexpected manner, love often comes in unexpected ways. He said that we don't always understand how or why God works the way He does, but that doesn't mean He isn't at work. That doesn't mean He doesn't love us. He stated that no one expected a tiny baby in a manger to one day save the world. No one saw it coming, but God had a plan. And He still has a plan.

I got it. I heard it. But it was all a blur, really. My heart was in such emotional turmoil that I heard the words he said—and, deep down, I knew that there was some truth to it. But I was just so darn angry. I couldn't get past myself. I couldn't. I didn't know how to feel any different.

The service ended with candlelight as we sang "Silent Night." I must admit it was beautiful. The church was beautiful. It took until the end of the service for me to notice the smell of the evergreens that hung from each stained glass window. There were four beautiful blue spruce trees at the front of the sanctuary and a big candlelit wreath with red ribbon above the baptistry. The tiny lights strung along the greenery and the candle lighting made the room glow with a warmth that brought a momentary peace to my soul.

I was glad that I had come for my mom. When I saw the smiles on her face and on Dad's afterward, I knew I had done the right thing. I hugged their necks and told them that I'd see them for lunch the next day. "I've got my dessert ready, and I'll be there a few minutes early to help set the table," I told them. We said our farewells, and I got in the car and headed home as quickly as I could get going.

Finally, I was out of there. It was over. I had done my part. Now, maybe, Mom would leave me alone for a while about church. I went straight home, popped some popcorn, and made some hot chocolate. I put on my softest pajamas and curled up with my dog, Keto. We snuggled up to watch another episode of my favorite show, *Friends*. I needed something to make me laugh. I had had enough tears and seriousness for the night. It was time to relax, unwind, and smile.

Chapter 6

HOME SWEET HOME

I must've been worn out from the stress of the evening because I don't think I ever made it to bed that night. I fell asleep right there in my recliner, curled up under a blanket to the glow of the television and the sounds of Monica, Chandler, Ross, Rachel, Joey, and Phoebe talking in the background. I was watching the one show that always made me laugh because I couldn't take any more sappy seriousness for the night—or for the next decade, for that matter. Keto had fallen asleep next to me and didn't bother to nudge me to go to bed. But really, I wouldn't have known it if he had. I was out for the count.

I woke up the next morning snuggled comfortably in my bed. The covers were all neatly tucked around me. My pillow was fluffed just right and positioned perfectly beneath my head. The bed smelled clean and fresh. My white comforter and eight-hundred-count sheets were newly washed and didn't have a wrinkle in them, and they felt silky on my legs. The feeling was like when you've just shaved your legs after a warm shower, dried off, put on lotion, and then go back to bed all clean and cozy.

I cuddled a little closer with my blankie that I'd had since I was a baby. It felt so good and squishy between my fingers. It was cool and cuddly on my cheek. I carried that thing around for years as a child. My family used to tease me about it, saying, "Are you gonna carry that thing around until your thirty?" It didn't bother me. I liked it, and I snuggled it. Honestly, I didn't even realize I still had it or where it had been for some time.

What a great feeling to wake up on Christmas morning and smell coffee brewing before you even have to get out of bed. I even smelled bacon, eggs, and biscuits coming from the kitchen. Momma's special Christmas breakfast—wait, what? After I realized what I was feeling and smelling, I opened my eyes and glanced around the room. How did I get in the bed last night? Did I sleepwalk? I must have because I don't remember coming to the bed. Keto, my mutt and the love of my life, wasn't lying on my legs or licking my face. Where was he?

I sat up and rubbed my eyes. I began to look around more carefully. This was my room, but it was my room from when I was a kid. What the heck? I was staring at my old bedroom. There were rainbow-colored curtains, Cabbage Patch dolls on the toy chest, and the little Care Bear lamp I once had, which was now sitting on the nightstand by my bed. My old blankie was lying over me, and it wasn't an old rag. It was perfectly sewn together the way it had been when I was a little girl. The pastel colors and patchwork, with the little elephant on the front, were back together as if the blanket had never been dragged around or slung from place to place.

I got out the of bed reluctantly and slid on my favorite unicorn slippers. Ha! "I used to love these things," I thought. "But how are my feet fitting in them now?" I stood up and noticed that I still had my favorite pajamas on from the night before. At least something was consistent. I walked over to the mirror and was relieved to find that I was still my real age, twenty-seven. Maybe this was a dream, and I was dreaming I was in a movie like *BIG* or *13 Going on 30*. It was the strangest thing, but my hair was perfectly in place. Not a strand needed brushing. My roots didn't need touching up, and my face was clear. No acne. No scars. No bags under my eyes. "Wow! I like this dream! I could get used to this," I told myself.

I looked down at my dresser and noticed my music box. I hadn't seen it in years. I turned the little key on the side a few times, and it began to play that song. "What was the name of it?" I thought to myself. "Oh! It's 'Memories'!" I loved it. Inside the box was a little place for jewelry, and I opened it just to see what was inside. I couldn't believe what I was seeing. It was my birthstone ring that Donnie had gotten me for Christmas when we were kids. It was a tiny pink stone in sterling silver that he had picked out just for me. I loved that thing. I wore it everywhere. I wouldn't take it off. In fact, the only time I ever did was the day I lost it. I was devastated.

My friends and I had been playing in the creek, swimming at a church picnic. I had taken it off and stuck it in my shoe to keep from losing or damaging it. When we got out to dry off, I accidentally knocked over the shoe when I grabbed my towel. I bent down to pick up my shoes and started walking toward the car. That's when I remembered that I had put the ring inside my shoe. It was too late! I had dropped the ring out on the ground somewhere, and I couldn't find where it had gone in the grass and rocks. My friends and family looked all over for it that day. I cried and cried, but we never found it. And yet, now, here it was! I picked it up, and tears welled up in my eyes. "Oh, Donnie," I sighed. I slid it on my pinkie finger. That's all it would fit now, but it fit my pinkie finger perfectly. This was definitely a good dream.

Since I was apparently not ready to wake up yet, I decided to see what else this dream would bring me. I followed my nose and headed to the kitchen. Sure enough, spread across the table was Christmas breakfast. Yum! It was beautiful, and it smelled delicious! Biscuits, gravy, and bacon, hmm! Mom must've been working all morning, I thought. She had even dragged out the fine china dishes.

I pulled a chair to the table and sat down to eat. Then it hit me: where was everybody? That's odd. Why would I be the only one here to enjoy Christmas breakfast? We hadn't really sat down together to have one since we lost Donald. If this was a dream, why couldn't Donnie be there? Where was he? Make him appear, Lizbeth; make him show up! It's your dream, dummy!

Chapter 7

BREAKFAST IS SERVED

I expected to wake up at any moment. I waited and waited for someone else to appear, but it was becoming increasingly more difficult to resist the food sitting in front of me. I decided I'd just go ahead and fix my plate. I mean, if no one else was going to eat, I might as well enjoy; it was my dream.

I pulled my biscuits apart. They were soft and flaky. They were still warm enough that I could see steam rising between each half as I set them on my plate. I used the butter knife on my Nana's butter dish to spread the butter across each piece. Momma had always used Nana's good Christmas china to celebrate on Christmas morning. She always made sure we had the best dishes ready to go along with a hot breakfast. Nana would've liked that.

I spooned gravy over each half of the biscuits. And as usual, I pulled apart one more biscuit. I spread it with butter and then Nana's grape jelly. I couldn't wait to dig in. I raised my first bite up to mouth but froze when I heard, "Aren't you gonna ask the blessing?"

"Nana?"

I turned around quickly. Sure enough, there stood Nana in her apron, standing in the kitchen with a dish towel in her hand. I dropped my fork and ran over to give her the biggest hug. "Nana!" I said. "What are you doing here? How are you …" I paused midquestion.

"Listen, child, I'm right where I'm supposed to be."

"But you … you're …"

"Dead? That's an expression we used to say back at our temporary home. Here, we realize there's no such thing as death."

"Here?"

Nana could tell I was confused. "Yes, child. Here in Heaven."

"Man, this is the coolest and craziest dream I've ever had," I thought to myself.

"I know. It's hard to wrap your mind around it, but it's true. This is just one small part of the happiest place you'll ever know."

"Disney World? Wait, no," I thought to myself. Then I was glad I didn't say it out loud. "Did I—" I was about to ask, but it was as if she could read my mind. Or at the very least, my thoughts were scrolling across my forehead.

"Die? No, honey, you're still alive and well." Nana smiled and patted my hand. She always used to do that. I forgot how much I missed my Nana hand pats.

"Then how? If I'm not there, and you're here, how can it be?"

"Isn't that the most amazing thing about our Heavenly Father, Lizbeth? With Him, it *can* be. It *can all* be."

"But I didn't think I was supposed to be able to come to Heaven unless I—"

"God's ways are not our ways, Lizbeth. He can see past the headlights. You know, you'll be driving along, seeing what you think is in front of you. You see what your lights show you. But God can see even further past those lights. He knows all the good, the bad, and everything between. Only He knows why you need this moment here with us."

"I have so many questions. I don't know where to start."

"Start with breakfast, child. You need your nourishment."

Nana and I sat down together at the table. She asked the blessing over the meal, and then she and I began to eat together. We hadn't done that in years. In fact, we had not done it since she passed. It felt amazing.

She hadn't changed a bit, except for maybe having a glow about her. She looked just as I remembered her in her prime, yet with a zest I don't think I ever knew. I listened as she talked about our family members as if she had been with us all along. It never occurred to me soon enough to ask, but how did she know what she knew? If she was gone, in Heaven, how did she know about my dad's new truck? How did she know Mom was working part time now and was semi-retired? It was crazy! Still, everything seemed perfectly normal—perfectly ... perfect!

"Let's go sit out on the front porch, Lizbeth."

I hadn't rocked on the front porch with my grandparents since I was a little kid. I was actually excited about it, though it was something that used to bore me to tears as a young child. Nana and I walked out to the front porch, and the strangest thing happened. As we stepped out of the kitchen and through the front door, we were no longer at my home where I grew up; we were now on Nana's front porch. The green-and-yellow daisy rockers were still there. I remember how clean they were. I was always amazed after becoming an adult that my Nana could keep her outdoor furniture so clean on her front porch. I looked out at the front lawn and saw her old bird bath. There were two red birds splashing and bathing in it.

When we sat, I looked ahead and down the drive. I could see mountain tops out in the distance. The sky was a pure blue, and the clouds were white and fluffy. The sun was shining brightly, but not blinding. The shade trees in her front yard were so green, and there was a gentle breeze blowing the branches back and forth. The grass looked like a bright-green carpet that had been rolled out as a welcome mat for all who visited. Nana's flowers were blooming: The rose bush was full of pink blossoms. The hydrangea bushes were full of lilac and white snowballs. The sweet aroma of the gardenias drifted up from the sides of the steps going down from the porch.

Now I knew. This was why they could sit there for hours. When I was finally sitting still and quiet, I could see the true beauty of all that was around me. God had so many gifts for me to see and enjoy, but I rarely slowed down long enough to appreciate them.

As I sat there close to Nana, I held her hand. I couldn't help but think of the last time I had seen her. It wasn't long before she had taken her last breath on earth. She wasn't in pain. It was just her time. She had been resting peacefully and was surrounded by her children and some of her grandkids. We were all truly blessed to have her. I remember kissing her on the forehead and telling her I loved her. I also remember leaning in for her to kiss me on the cheek, and she did. She told me she loved me too. I had wondered then if it would be the last time I saw her.

"Nana, I love you," I said as I leaned over on her shoulder.

"I love you too, Lizbeth," she said. She wrapped her arms around me.

"This is the best day ever!"

"Every day is the best day here, child."

"Do you every wish—"

"No, Lizbeth. I have never been happier. You don't know what life is all about until you see the other side of it, love, and the way it's meant to be."

"Well, how is it that I'm here? I mean, if I'm not … gone."

"That's not for me to say. Our Father has plans we know nothing about, and He doesn't waste an opportunity."

"You mean there's a lesson for me to learn?"

"Maybe. Only God knows, child."

"Can I see Him? Here in Heaven?"

"Oh, Lizbeth, you will most definitely see God in Heaven. It may not be the way you expect, but you will see God in Heaven."

"But …"

"Rest, child. Let's just enjoy the moment."

We rocked and hugged one another, and before I knew it, I had drifted off to sleep just like I had when I was a child, rocking in her lap.

Chapter 8

LITTLE MIRACLES

I woke up to the sound of children playing and squealing. I had rested so well and had fallen asleep in the rocker sitting on my Nana's front porch. When I sat up, I noticed there was a playground in front of me. It had slides, swings, monkey bars, and seesaws. Children were running and playing. They squealed with excitement as they played together and ran from place to place. One can't help but smile when you hear the continuous giggle of a child. It's like listening to a baby's belly laugh. It's contagious. And here, in this place, there were giggles and squeals. They were having a good time.

Oddly, I realized there were many children playing but no adults around. My instincts as a woman kicked in, I guess. I looked around to see who was watching after them. I decided to take a seat on a park bench nearby and just watch them, until whoever was supposed to be with them returned. I hadn't been there long when a lady came over and sat down beside me.

"Hello," I said, trying to be polite.

"Hi," she said as she hesitantly smiled.

As I looked at her, I realized that I recognized her. She and her husband went to my mom's church. In fact, she had been at the Christmas Eve service the night before sitting in front of us.

"Don't you go to Friendship Baptist Church?" I asked.

"Yes, I do," she replied.

"I'm Bryant and Louise Webb's daughter, Lizbeth. They attend there as well," I shared, reaching out to shake her hand.

"That's right. I'm Susan Brown. It's nice to meet you."

For a minute, I guess I forgot where I was. I was carrying on a regular conversation with another human whom I had just seen the night before. She was also alive and well.

"They're so cute, aren't they?"

"Yes. I couldn't help but make my way over to watch them play."

"I know. I wondered who might be watching them. I didn't see anyone else around until you came along."

"Oh, that's true. They remind me of when I was little. I remember swinging as high as I could on the swings at our school. Feeling the breeze in my hair and on my skin was as close to flying as a little girl could get."

"Yes! Me too." I looked over and noticed that the swings had a few openings. "Hey, there are a few swings free. Do you wanna go over and play like old times?" I wondered if she thought I was crazy. Here was a grown woman introducing herself for the first time, and the first thing she was asked to do was to go play on the swings with a total stranger.

"Sure! Why not?"

We got up and walked over to the swings. Each of us took a seat in one. I noticed a little blonde-headed girl next to the one I sat in. She was cute! She had pigtails with pink and white ribbons and a pink dress with the cutest little striped leggings.

"Hi," she said.

"Hi there," I replied, surprised that she would talk to an adult coming over to intrude on her play space.

"What's your name?" she asked.

"My name is Lizbeth. What's your name?"

"My name is Faith."

"Faith, may I swing with you?"

"Yes! I love to swing!"

"Me too. I love your pink dress too."

"Thank you!" She giggled and laughed as we started to go back and forth. I felt the wind beneath me, and I started to giggle too. Susan did as well. We were all swinging and giggling like little children. I felt the warmth of what felt like the sunshine on a spring day. There was light, but it wasn't exactly sunlight. Yet it lit up the outdoors like sunshine. I could smell fresh flowers blooming. It looked like Easter as I glanced around because there were tulips, hyacinths, and daffodils growing all around the playground. I couldn't help but want to just sniff them. I put my feet down and slowed my swing so it could stop.

"I have to go take a look at these pretty flowers, ladies," I told Faith and Susan.

"I'll come too," Susan said.

"Me too," Faith said eagerly.

We walked over together and knelt to smell them.

"You can pick them. They grow back," Faith told us.

"The pink ones smell the best." She picked a pink hyacinth and handed it to me.

"It's so pretty here, Faith. Who are you here with?" I asked her.

"You, silly," she said as she giggled.

Susan and I both laughed and grinned at one another. "No, I mean who is taking care of you?"

Faith looked at me as if I had asked the silliest question ever. "God. God always watches over us."

It occurred to me that I was still in Heaven. Duh, Lizbeth! I was just about to continue our conversation when I heard the squeal of another little girl who was running up behind us.

"Mommy! Mommy! Mommy," the little girl exclaimed.

"Mommy?" I wondered. "Who was this kid talking to?" Then when I turned around, I saw her.

A little brown-haired girl with short curls, fair skin, and tiny freckles on her nose ran straight up to Susan and threw her arms around her waist. She hugged her as tightly as one could. Susan froze, and the strangest thing happened next. She bent down and looked directly into the hazel eyes of this bubbly little girl.

"Mariel?" Susan asked.

"Hi, Mommy! You came to play with me," the little angel exclaimed.

Tears welled up in Susan's eyes, and she threw her arms around this precious child. "Oh yes, baby! I did. I came to play with you today! Oh my goodness! I can't believe it! You're alive! You're all right! Are you okay, baby?"

"Yes, Mommy. I'm okay. Let's play! Let's play! Let's

play," Mariel said as she held Susan's hands and jumped up and down.

For the next few hours, I played with several tiny children and watched Susan play with her little girl. I don't know that I'd ever had so much fun, even as a child myself. We swang on the swings. We slid down the slides. We climbed on the monkey bars. We played hopscotch. We lay in the grassy field and wildflowers, looking up at the clouds and guessing the passing shapes they made. We rode the merry-go-round and seesaw. We rolled down the grassy hills from top to bottom. We picked flowers and made bouquets for one another. After a game of leapfrog, I walked back over to the park bench.

I don't know that I'd ever seen anything more beautiful. Susan and Mariel were the happiest two people who could ever be. They walked hand in hand. They sang a sweet little silly song that they both clearly knew. It was something about a teddy bear and a picnic. They were clearly in Heaven just being with one another.

As I was admiring it all, I heard church bells play "Jesus Loves Me" nearby. The children heard it too, and at once, they all came down from the playground equipment and began to wave good-bye, run, skip, and gallop over to a white gate near a beautiful flower garden. I glanced over to Susan and noticed Mariel hugging her neck again. They embraced for a moment and took one last, long look into one another's eyes. Mariel kissed Susan on the cheek and then ran to the gate after the other little ones. The gate closed, and the noise of giggly children that had filled the air was gone. It was quiet. Only the sound of birds chirping occasionally was left.

As Susan walked over to me, I prepared myself to comfort her. I had no idea what to say or do. I had no idea how she knew this child, or worse, what had happened if Mariel was calling her *Mommy*. It was none of my business, but here we were. Before today, I knew nothing about this stranger from my mom's church. Yet now, I knew something very personal. I was trying to figure out what to do if she fell apart on me when she sat down next to me.

"Are you okay?" I asked.

"I've … literally never been better," she replied.

Well, I didn't expect her to say that. "Great," I said hesitantly. I was trying to wrap my mind around everything that had just happened. "Mariel's your daughter?"

"Yes," Susan answered with a smile.

"What happened? I mean … I'm sorry. I don't mean to be too forward. How old was she? Ugh. Nothing I'm saying is coming out right."

"It's okay. Your questions don't bother me at all. My husband and I tried to get pregnant for two and half years with no success. The day I found out I was pregnant, I was shocked. I couldn't believe it had actually happened. I was too excited to surprise Kyle. I told him right after I took a test. We were beside ourselves.

"We started teasing one another about baby names. If it was a boy, we wanted to name him Mark Kyle after my dad and after Kyle. If it was a girl, I wanted to name her Ariel, and he wanted to name her Mary. We teasingly argued about it and agreed on a compromise of Mariel if we found out the baby was, in fact, a girl.

"We made the doctor's appointment to confirm the pregnancy as soon as we found out from our home test. I figured I was about six and a half weeks when we called. They let me come in for a blood test to affirm, but they didn't typically book the first visit until between eight and ten weeks, so we had to wait a little while for our first ultrasound. We were so excited and nervous. Waiting for it was driving us crazy. Our little name game kept us busy while we waited. It was our little secret. We planned to surprise our folks at Thanksgiving dinner. It would fall about a week after our appointment, and we'd have our first ultrasound pictures to share.

"I remember the day like it was yesterday. We both took off work, and Kyle had his phone ready to record our first moment seeing our baby for the first time. As the ultrasound tech was punching in keys on the keyboard, she stared at the screen for several seconds that seemed like an eternity. Kyle squeezed my hand and grinned.

"The ultrasound tech continued to explore the images, and she remained quiet. I finally asked the question that was starting to creep into my mind. 'Is everything okay?' The lady explained to us that she wasn't picking up a heartbeat. She said it could be that the conception date may have been miscalculated. It could be too soon to pick up a heartbeat. She took the images and planned to share the results with the doctor. Then she told me that I could get dressed and that the doctor would meet me shortly after to discuss our next steps.

"I was told to come back in one to two weeks for another ultrasound to see how things had progressed. We made our next appointment exactly one and a half weeks from that day and made sure we were both able to be there again.

Naïvely, we believed every hopeful word the doctor had given us.

"We were back in the same room again with the same ultrasound tech. She was again looking at the screen and snapping images quietly as Kyle and I squeezed one another's hands tightly.

"'I'm still not getting a heartbeat,' she said. 'Let me go see if Dr. King is available. Maybe he can look while we are in here.' At this point, we were starting to get nervous. Not seeing a heartbeat couldn't be a good thing. But then again, why were we seeing the image of something on the screen? Clearly, something was there. We thought.

"Dr. King came in within a few minutes, but it felt like forever. After looking at the images, he sat down next to us and explained that the something we saw in the images appeared to be a blighted ovum. Apparently, that meant that a fetus had started to develop, but the development never completed for whatever reason. He explained that I would likely miscarry in the coming weeks.

"We were absolutely devastated. All the hopes and plans we had for our first pregnancy were crushed in one moment. What was meant to be a surprise for our family ended up being a prayer request and a heartbreaking moment for our entire family.

"To make matters worse, my body would not naturally release the 'tissue' as they called it. They had to schedule a DNC for me. I went through the procedure and recovery. Kyle and I grieved together, but we could feel the prayers of our loved ones even though we were heartbroken.

"After the procedure, I kept bleeding. It had been weeks, and I continued to bleed. We contacted the doctor's office to confirm that this was normal. They asked me to come in again for a visit. Once again, we found ourselves in the ultrasound room. They discovered that not all of the tissue had been removed because the first procedure was done blindly—or something along those lines. Part of it was lingering in my uterus, which was causing me to continue to bleed.

"Not only was our first and only pregnancy devastating, the loss was never-ending. I was just ready for it all to be over and to be back to my normal self. We couldn't and wouldn't try again for about a year. Finally, we started trying again last year, but we haven't had any success."

"Oh, Susan. I'm so sorry. Today must've been terribly difficult for you," I was in tears myself.

"Actually, it was quite the opposite," she said. "It was the most beautiful and wonderful day of my life. I only wish that Kyle could have been here with me. I looked into my child's eyes, and she was absolutely perfect. She is a child. She was a child. She was real. She wasn't just a blighted ovum. She wasn't a mistake. She was my child. She is my child. More importantly, she is a child of God. He didn't hurt her or harm her. He was holding her safely in His arms the whole time. She is our little Mariel, our miracle."

Susan and I hugged again. Although really, we'd just met, we had talked and held one another like we'd been friends for years. She felt like family now.

Chapter 9

DANCING IN HEAVEN

*S*usan and I walked and talked. We carried on like sisters. We didn't even notice that the sun was starting to set. The sky was filled with the most brilliant colors of orange, pink, yellow, purple, and blue. It was more beautiful than any sunset or painting I'd ever seen. Words can't express how amazing the colors were, swirled and faded together—almost like a rainbow but even more brilliant.

As we walked, we heard some music playing and the sounds of laughter. We noticed that, as we followed the path before us, it led to a large white tent that was lit up and had people inside. Outdoor lighting had been strung around the tent's perimeter. It was very pretty in the dim light of the evening. We approached the tent to see what the occasion was. Inside, people appeared to be celebrating with food, music, dancing, and laughter. They were dressed in nice clothing. I assumed it was some sort of wedding reception or something to that effect.

We were peeking around the corner when a lady wearing a flowing, ivory dress approached us. She was very attractive and seemed to be glowing as she handed us each a glass of punch.

"Oh, thank you," we both replied, surprised. We stepped inside the tent.

I leaned in and whispered to Susan. "What's the occasion?"

"I have no idea," she whispered back. We both chuckled and took a sip of our punch. We happily joined the celebration and danced along with everyone else. We had such a good time. It was as if we'd known these people all along. It was as if the party was for us!

Suddenly, as a song we were dancing to ended, a gentleman went up to a microphone on the stage. "Good evening, everyone! We are so glad you are here to celebrate the lives of our fellow believers, the sons and daughters of Christ Jesus, our Lord," he exclaimed.

"Amen," everyone shouted and clapped.

"Is this place Pentecostal?" I wondered. I clapped right along with everyone, though, because a person becoming a believer is a wonderful thing. I wondered who they might be welcoming.

"At this time, we are going to welcome one of our beautiful young ladies to the dance floor. Melody, why don't you come on over, sweetheart?"

I looked around for the young lady named Melody. The crowd that was gathered sort of parted down the middle. A girl wearing a pretty purple dress, seated in a wheelchair, rolled through to the center of the circle that had formed around the dance floor. Everyone clapped as she entered.

She looked strangely familiar to me. I felt like I had seen her somewhere before.

She had long, sandy-brown hair with curls and a white ribbon pulling half of her hair off her face. She had the prettiest little pearl earrings in her ears, and her cheeks had a natural glow about them. There were tiny freckles on her nose and cheeks, and her lips shined as if she had put just a tiny bit of light-pink gloss on them. She appeared to be about thirteen years old. She beamed as they applauded her during her entrance. She was radiant. Everyone admired her the way one admires a bride coming down the aisle in a wedding.

"Melody, we welcome you," the announcer exclaimed.

Then, unexpectedly, a dove flew down from somewhere and landed on the arm of her wheelchair. She began to glow like there was an aura around her silhouette. I wondered if I was imagining this. I questioned the reality of it all and wondered whether I was officially off my rocker at that point. And suddenly, there was a voice in the air that was calm and deep. It wasn't the announcer this time. Softly and peacefully, it spoke five simple words.

"Get up. Walk, my child," the voice said.

A gentleman standing next to the girl bent down and folded in the footrests of her chair. Without hesitation, Melody stood up. She smiled and took a deep breath. Then she stepped forward. She was barefoot, and as her toes reached the floor, she put her weight down on the rest of her foot like a dancer as she took her first step. Then she took another step. And another, and another. Then she turned, looked up, and smiled. Her grin stretched from ear to ear!

The dove flew up into the sky past her, and music

began to play on what sounded like a piano. It was a song I recognized. It was a beautiful song. I soon realized that it was "I Can Only Imagine," by Mercy Me. And then, I couldn't believe my eyes. Something incredible happened!

Melody, the young lady we'd been watching, began to dance. She danced as if her legs had always worked wonderfully. She glided, turned, and leapt across the dance floor like a well-trained ballerina. Every time she jumped into the air, it seemed as if she was flying. She spun with such grace that it appeared she had danced for years—or professionally, for that matter. I had taken dance classes as a child, and I can tell you that I would have only dreamed of dancing the way she did at her age.

As the song came to an end, everyone clapped and cheered. Melody curtsied and then ran to an older woman nearby, whom I assume was a relative, and hugged her neck. Tears of joy flowed from their eyes. It was a miracle! I had witnessed a true miracle! I really must be in Heaven. But how?

Chapter 10

TOGETHER AGAIN

I realized I had gotten separated from Susan. "Where did she go?" I asked myself, but before my thoughts could continue, the announcer came back to the microphone.

"That was absolutely wonderful, Melody! We are so glad that we could share in your special moment," he continued. "Now, we're going to honor two very special people at this time. This is something that's been a long time coming. Daryl, please welcome your bride, Mrs. Angeline."

"Oh! This must be the real occasion! It's a wedding celebration after all," I thought to myself. "But hold on. Why would they feature a little girl? Was she family? Who are these people, and how do I know them well enough to be invited to their wedding reception?"

Just then, an older man, tall and slender with salt-and-pepper hair, stepped forward. He appeared to be in his early sixties. He wore a navy suit with a matching tie and looked very nice. I could smell a hint of what seemed to be a familiar cologne or aftershave. It was something like the one my uncle used to wear. He, too, looked so happy—just like Melody had a few moments before.

The man named Daryl reached out his hand, and the crowd parted again for a pretty lady wearing a blue floral dress. The skirt of her dress appeared to blow gently in a breeze that came through the tent at that very moment. Her hair was short and dark brown, with curls. Her eyes were a dark shade of blue that matched her dress perfectly. She, too, appeared to be in her sixties or late fifties. She had an engaging smile that was contagious to anyone who looked at her. Everyone around them was in awe.

The announcer spoke again as the couple walked toward one another and then embraced in joyful tears. It looked as if they were having a reunion of sorts, as if they hadn't seen one another in a very long time. "Daryl and Angeline, we know that cancer took its toll on you both for many years. It separated you long ago and left you heartbroken, Angeline. Here, I can tell you that there are no more tears. There is no more pain, no more heartache, and no more sickness. You can gladly stand hand in hand with your dear husband, knowing he will no longer be weak. He will no longer be winded or too tired to stand. His body is strong again. His energy has returned. There will be no more nausea, no medications to remember or worry about, no more doctor visits, and no more medical bills to pay. You are finally, truly at home with the love of your life."

They joined together and danced as another familiar song played. It was the "Tennessee Waltz." They were so sweet as they waltzed across the dance floor. No one could help but shed tears at this most precious and momentous occasion. What a blessing to be reunited with a spouse who had passed! Happiness was everywhere! As the couple finished, the announcer came back to the mic and told everyone to enjoy themselves and the refreshments provided. There was plenty for everyone.

I looked for Susan and continued to mingle with folks, but I couldn't find her anywhere. I hoped she hadn't missed the party. It was amazing! People started to depart from the reception. I decided I would head back to the old house and take a rest. I felt like a good night's sleep would be wonderful. I wasn't really tired, but I loved the way it felt to snuggle up under the covers of my old bed with my favorite pillow. I thought it would be nice to tell Nana all about my day. Maybe she could tell me who everyone was. I knew their faces, but I couldn't place them all.

I made it back to my old home and saw that the porch light was on at the screened-in porch. It looked just like it did when I was a little girl. I decided to sit down in the rocker for old times' sake. I propped my feet up like I had when I was a kid. As I sat there, it began to rain. There was a soft breeze, and the pitter patter of rain falling on the roof was soothing and relaxing. I rocked and listened to the droplets. I smelled the fresh rain as it replenished the flowers, plants, and trees around the house. Everything was in bloom and so pretty in Momma and Daddy's flower garden. The trees and grass were the most striking shade of green. Even by the light of the moon, I could see the water shining on the leaves and blades of grass.

"Is that you, Lizbeth?" Nana called from inside.

"Yes, Nana," I said. "I'll be in shortly. I've got so much to tell you!"

Today had been one of the best days of my life. I smiled, leaned my head back on the cushion of the rocker, and began to yawn. The sound of the rain and the rocking was putting me to sleep just like it did when I was little girl, and Momma would rock me in her arms during a rain. Before I knew it, I had drifted off into a deep sleep right there.

Chapter 11

WHY

I woke up the next morning thinking I'd be in my own bed and awakened to the reality that my day in Heaven had been only a dream. To my surprise, however, I woke to the smell of another wonderful breakfast, just like on Christmas! I was still in the rocker on the porch, so I went inside and told Nana all about the previous day. She and I enjoyed each other's company like we never had before. We connected in a new way. We were not only grandchild and grandmother, but friends—sisters, even. I was treasuring every second of our chat and soaking up every word. As I watched her sip her coffee, she got quiet and grinned.

"What is it, Nana? What's on your mind?" I asked.

"I haven't seen you this happy in a long time, doll. I'm happy that you're happy," she answered and smiled.

"I've tried, Nana. I really have. It's just that, after losing Donnie and you, I just … couldn't. I still don't understand. I mean …" I hesitated.

"Why?" she asked.

"Well, yes! Why did he have to go? Why did both of you have to go so soon? We could have been so close, you and I. Donnie and I were so close. It just wasn't—"

"Fair," she finished my sentence. I nodded in agreement.

"His life was cut so short. He was just getting started."

"Lizbeth, why not you? Why not me? Why not Donald? For that matter, why Jesus? Why was his life taken at only around thirty-three years? Some might say He still had a lot of life to live and a lot of good to do."

"I don't really know," I said reluctantly.

"Lizbeth, you're not God. Frankly, child, you don't know it all. There's no way you could make sense of this world that sin has made a mess of for us all. Sometimes you just have to trust the Lord with all your strength and with all your might, and lean not on your own understanding, as the scripture says."

"That's Daddy's favorite verse."

"Yes, and he knows what it means to truly trust the Lord."

"I know. I don't know how he or Momma does it. He's never questioned it."

"Well, sure he has! He just doesn't let you see it. But he's human, just like you and me. He's struggled in his own way. He has had to deal with it in his own way. We all handle things differently. But, Lizbeth, your daddy learned a long time ago that to survive, he had to surrender his hurt to God. He had to let God have his hurt and pain so that healing could take place. As long as your father held on to the anger, sadness, and heartache, he could not have any peace.

"He had to accept that Donald was not in pain. Donald was not in harm's way. He didn't have to wonder because he knew Donald was a Christian. He was safe in the arms of His Heavenly Father. Donnie had merely been on loan to your daddy."

I chuckled. "You called him *Donnie*. That's what we all used to call him."

"I know, sugar. I know."

Of course she did. Nana seemed to know everything, and she was right. She knew better than me for sure. For the first time ever, I was able to accept it all a little better.

"I think it's time for you to go to the diner."

"But we just ate."

"Oh, I know, but there's something you need to do."

"Well, let me help you clean up first, Nana."

"No, no. You go on ahead and get to the diner. They're waiting for you."

"Okay," I said with pause. I wondered who was waiting for me now.

This was all a lot to take in. So much information, so much to process. So much to accept. This dream was kicking my butt. "When are you gonna wake up?" I thought to myself.

I headed out the door to the side porch and walked down the road in front of the house. The sun was shining, and birds were chirping. It was a comfortable temperature of what felt like about seventy-two degrees. I noticed a rabbit hopping along next to me as I walked. It didn't appear to be frightened by me as most wild animals do. Again today, I could hear what sounded like church bells in the distance. The ringing reminded me of our church on Sunday mornings when I was little. As I followed the road, my familiar surroundings changed into something new and different.

I passed a creek with wildflowers growing all around it. It was like a patchwork quilt of color stretched all along the creekside. I crossed a little white bridge that went over the creek and looked over the side to see fish swimming in the stream below. As I walked, I realized I was making my way into a small town. There was a post office, a flower shop, a barber shop, and a grocery store, among other things. It was like Mayberry from *The Andy Griffith Show* that Mom and Dad used to watch with us on family movie nights.

I soon smelled the aroma of fresh-grilled hamburgers. Yum! I wasn't hungry, but, man, something smelled good. As I rounded the corner, I saw a neon sign for a small restaurant that said DINER. "That must be the place," I thought. I walked over to the front door. I had no clue what was in store for me next.

Chapter 12

THE DINER

I stepped inside the diner and looked around. I wasn't sure where I should sit or if I was supposed to seat myself.

"Just seat yourself, honey," a lady at the counter in a waitress outfit called out to me. She reminded me of Dolly Parton with her southern drawl, blonde hair, and petite frame. She smiled. "I'll bring ya a cup of coffee in a jiffy. Two sugars and one cream, right, baby?"

"Yes, ma'am," I said with surprise. Wow! She knew I liked coffee, and she knew how I liked it. "No wonder Nana recommended I come here," I thought as I grinned and giggled to myself.

I chose to sit at a booth facing the front windows. The kitchen and bar were on the other side of the booths to my right, so I could still see the friendly waitress as she headed my way. But I could also see the amazing view of this quaint little Mayberry-like town.

I was people-watching as the waitress came up to my

table with the coffee. "Here's your coffee, Lizbeth, just the way you like it," she said.

"Awesome! Thank you," I replied as I stared at her. "I'm sorry. I can't help but think that you remind me so much of someone famous from back home, where I live. Has anyone ever told you that you look very much like Dolly Parton?"

The lady just heehawed back at me. "Well, darlin', that might be because I am Dolly Parton," she said as she pointed to her name tag on her uniform.

"Really? Truly? I'm talking to the actual, real-live Dolly Parton?"

"Last time I checked, that's what my nametag said." She continued to giggle at me.

"But you're a waitress? In a diner? Shouldn't someone else be waiting on you?"

"Actually, honey, it's quite the opposite." She turned to speak to a gentleman coming through the door. "I'll be right with ya, Herb. Black coffee comin' your way!" She turned back to me. "I'll be right back with a piece of homemade apple pie and ice cream and explain everything to ya. Okay, sweetheart? Sounds like you and I need to have a little girl talk, heart to heart."

"Sure!" I still couldn't believe it. I was seeing Dolly Parton face to face. She was my waitress, and she was going to sit down and talk to me! This was all so surreal. I continued to sip my coffee and people-watch. I couldn't help but stare at Dolly as she waited on the customers and helped them with such kindness and happiness. Everyone here seemed so nice!

Finally, she returned to my booth. "All right, chickadee. let's talk!"

I was giddy with excitement as she sat down with two plates full of apple pie and ice cream. It wasn't just the food I was excited about; it was the company! I was starstruck!

"Lizbeth, I'm so glad to see you, and I can see that you're happy to be here. It may surprise you to see me as a waitress, but the truth is, I always like helping people. I love talking to folks about their day, hearing about their families, and making people laugh. Being a country music star is wonderful! I love every minute of it. But here, I really get to interact with people. I can really get to know them."

"But you are just so talented! It's so hard to imagine you waiting on anyone. How does a Grammy- and Academy Award–winning artist end up working as a waitress in a diner?"

"God calls us all to serve, Lizbeth. Serving one another is part of loving one another. I can sing about love all day long, but until I really love on others, I don't really know what I'm singing about. Ya see, sometimes you've got to help another to help yourself."

"Does it bother you? Working so hard as a waitress." I couldn't believe I was asking Dolly Parton these questions.

"No, honey, not at all! I love people, and I love to talk. And I get to do what God calls us all to do. Love my neighbors and serve them with gladness! Now, I've gotta get back to work. You go on and enjoy that pie because calories don't count in Heaven," she said with a wink as she slid out of the booth.

I ate my pie and ice cream. I sipped my coffee. I was just finishing up and wiping my mouth with a napkin when I saw a blue Volkswagen bug pull into the diner parking lot. I watched as a guy wearing a flannel shirt got out of the car. Then, I heard the doorbell ring as he entered the diner.

Chapter 13

PRICELESS

*T*he person who came inside was a young man about my age. He scanned the diner before he moved in, and then he looked my direction. But before he could move, he was stopped in his tracks as Dolly walked over and hugged his neck. She patted him on the back and told him that it was good to see him. Then she pointed over my way. Sure enough. He headed over to my booth and stood in front of me. I looked away as if I was trying not to stare, but then he spoke.

"Lizbeth."

That voice ... I looked up. It couldn't be ... could it?

"Donnie?"

"Get up here and give me a hug, you brat!"

I jumped up and threw my arms around him. He hugged me, and I knew that smell. It smelled like his cologne and deodorant right after he'd taken a shower and gotten ready for a date. I didn't wanna let go.

"Is it really you, Donnie? I've waited so long just to hear your voice."

"It's me in the spirit!" He laughed.

"Sit down! Have some apple pie. It's delicious, by the way!"

"Yeah, I know! Dolly takes good care of me."

"Can you believe Dolly Parton works here as a waitress?"

"Pretty cool, right?"

"Donnie," I began to get choked up. "I've missed you so much!"

"I know, Lizzie Lizard."

"Oh, goodness! I forgot that you called me that. It doesn't even bother me anymore."

"You used to hate it."

"Yes, I did. But now I'd give anything just to hear your voice, Bubba. Are you okay? Do you need anything? How are you feeling?"

"Lizzie, I'm in Heaven. How do think I'm feeling? I've got free food, apple pie, and ice cream, and I'll never gain weight. I've got it made here."

We both laughed for what seemed like a full minute.

"Those Webb kids are getting a little too rowdy over there, Herb! We may have to throw them out," Dolly teased.

We grinned and carried on as usual. It was just like old times, as if no time had passed.

"Did it hurt … when you had the accident?" I asked reluctantly.

"No, actually. I don't remember any of it. I just remember reaching for something, and then everything went dark, and then it got light again. Bright light! And then I was here, and there was this party and all."

"A party? Were you scared?"

"Not at all. In fact, I've never felt better. I know that you all are okay, so I don't have to worry about anything. God is in control."

"Do you know why He had to take you? Why it couldn't have been me instead?"

"Lizzie, only God knows why He allows certain things to happen. But I do know that I've never once looked back. Everything here seems right. I have peace that I never knew on Earth. An angel told me one time that God sometimes needs people here to help Him too. He said we've got special jobs to do here that are just as important as the ones on earth, if not more."

"What is your job here?"

"I'm a mechanic. I work on cars and machines—anything that has a motor, really."

"Oh, wow! That's right up your alley. I bet you love that!"

"I do! The coolest part is that when I got here, it's like I instantly became an expert at it. It's like God took my talents, gifts, and special interests, and just allowed me to know all there was to know to be able to help someone."

"That's great, Donnie! I am so happy to hear that. I'm so happy for you!"

"Aah," Donnie grunted, grinned, and tucked his chin down shyly.

Dolly brought us a refill of coffee. It was hot and steamy, but amazingly, it didn't burn to the touch. It was another great benefit of being in Heaven, I assume.

"Mom and Dad miss you terribly. I know they wish they could have said or done something—"

Donnie interrupted me. "There's nothing that will stop God's plans, Lizzie. He makes no mistakes. Satan is a little punk! He likes to throw lies our way and get inside our heads to make us think we can do something to alter the course of the universe. He enjoys watching people suffer in guilt and anger.

"Unfortunately, there's nothing we can do here to change the course for those who torture themselves on earth. It's their own road to walk, and that path is between them and God alone. We can pray for them, and we do. When they're able to turn it over to God, He will and does set them free.

"You see, here, there is no Satan. Shame, guilt, regret, and anger have no place. In Heaven, they simply don't exist. And I cannot wait for Mom and Dad to experience such peace and joy!" He squeezed my hand. "Lizzie, Mom and Dad are where they need to be. I wanna make sure that you get it. There's nothing that can change the way things are meant to be. And while you're on Earth, you may never see the why or reason for it all. But there will be a day when it all makes sense. We just have to trust and wait for God to finish our puzzles."

"I think I'm starting to see that," I said.

"Come on. I wanna show ya something." Donnie got up from the booth and motioned for me to follow him.

"Bye, Dolly," I exclaimed as we headed out of the diner.

"Bye, sweetie! And y'all come back now, ya hear?" she shouted.

We laughed and headed out the door to Donald's car. It was the same car that he had been driving when he wrecked. I hesitated at the passenger door.

"What?" he asked.

"Donnie, it's the—"

"I told you, Lizzie. Nothing is as it seems. Now, come on!"

I opened the door and took a deep breath. I got inside and reminded myself that nothing had been as it seemed during this entire journey. And, truly, there had been nothing to worry about. Everything was perfect in its own time. Just as God intended, I guess.

I looked over at the ignition. "You still have that keychain?" I asked. It was an old rabbit's foot that my uncle had given him when we were younger.

"Yeah, pretty cool, right?" he responded.

"I forgot about that thing."

Donnie drove us to a beautiful mountain. It reminded me of the Foothills Parkway back home in the Great Smokey Mountains. The leaves were full of color like they are in fall. It was the painting of the master artist, indeed. As we rounded up the mountain top, I noticed the views kept getting better and better.

"Where are we going?" I asked.

"You'll see, Lizzie. You'll see," Donnie replied.

A few minutes later, we made it to a viewpoint. There was a huge sign at the lookout that said, "The Window." I thought that was a strange name for a mountaintop, but who was I to judge? So far, I had discovered how little I really knew.

Donnie parked the car and started to get out. "Come on, sis," he told me.

I opened the door and stepped outside the car. Donnie led us over to an area that looked like stadium seating made from river rock—huge river rocks. It was cool! We took a seat, and Donnie stared straight ahead.

"Dude! Donnie, you're zoning." I waved my hand in front of his eyes and looked out across the horizon. "Is there something I'm missing?"

"Just wait. I told ya, you've gotta learn to trust and know when to wait for the Lord."

We sat there for a couple of minutes, but what felt like an eternity to me. I was shocked that Donnie could sit still that long. This was a totally different side of him. Sitting still? Waiting patiently? Telling me to be calm? We were definitely in another universe!

Just when I was about to get up and move around—I have trouble sitting still sometimes too—the view in front of us changed from beautiful mountain scenery to what appeared to be a huge picture window. It was almost like a movie screen, just for us! It faded into focus before our eyes. It was almost like seeing one's reflection in water, starting somewhat distorted, and then settling into focus.

"What's happening?" I asked.

"You'll see." Donald nudged me and grinned.

Just then, an image appeared on the screen. I saw a woman walk up to an older gentleman. She appeared to be in her forties. He looked to be in his early seventies. His hair was white, but he didn't have the stoop or walk of a man his age. He stood straight and strong. As the lady approached, she began to run toward him, faster and faster. Soon, she threw her arms around the older man. He hugged her back and swung her around in a circle. He put her down, and they started to talk.

"Daddy, I've missed you so much," the woman exclaimed.

"Now we can have that dance we've both been waiting for! Just like when you were a little girl," the man replied.

They began to dance together.

"What happened to him?" I asked Donnie.

Donnie pointed to the window. It showed a picture of a young man putting together a crib while his wife stood by, smiling. Then, it faded to a picture of the daughter and her father. He was rocking her in a rocking chair and singing her a lullaby. Next, it showed him lifting his little girl up to shoot a basketball into the goal. The window faded from the basketball court to him handing her a set of keys standing next to a car with a big red bow across the hood. He scooped the daughter up just like the older gentleman had.

From there, the picture faded to a scene of the man walking his daughter down the aisle at her wedding and giving her away to her groom. It then showed the gentleman starting to look a bit older, bouncing a little boy who was clearly his grandchild on his knee. His daughter looked on with such pride at both of them. And then we saw the man showing his grandson how to drive a tractor. Both grandson and grandpa were beaming.

The next scene was a little different. The older gentleman wasn't feeling well, and then they were in a doctor's office with his wife and his children. The doctor was breaking the news to them. It was cancer. They had found it and were going to begin a treatment plan. The doctor's office soon became a chemo treatment facility. The older gentleman was hooked up to an IV. The daughter drove them home, but they had to stop because he was so nauseated. Finally, he lay in a hospital bed, weak and frail. His daughter held his hand, and other family members stood gathered around him. They soon were gathered around a gravesite. There were tears and hugs. It was clear that this poor man had suffered near the end of his life.

"He was so sick," I told Donnie.

Donnie turned to me. "He was. Yet, he had such a lasting impact on his daughter and his loved ones. And now, he doesn't suffer anymore."

"It's like Heaven is one big family reunion."

"It's exactly that, except the kind you don't wanna miss." Donnie laughed.

I laughed too. "Is that all Heaven is about?"

"You're asking the wrong guy. And no. There's always more here."

"Who do I ask …" I trailed off in my question as Donnie gave me a smirk. "Oh, right," I said, blushing a little bit.

"Keep watching." Donnie pointed back to the window.

The picture changed again. This time, it showed the life of an older lady. She was in a house alone and eating a meal—supper, perhaps. She had two places set at the table, but she was the only one there. She said her blessing and began to eat. It continued by showing her writing and addressing cards and envelopes. With each one she wrote, she would close and sign, "God bless you, Judy." She walked slowly and wobbly to the mailbox, but she went each day. It showed her in the pew at church and walking slowly to her car each week afterward.

Next, the window showed a funeral for her. It wasn't much, and there weren't many people physically there, but it was nice. The sound of an old hymn, "I'll Fly Away," began to play. Then, the older lady was standing next to be what must've been an angel. He had his arm around her shoulders as he stood at her side. He had a glow about him. He had such a kind smile.

Dozens of people walked up to them. They were coming to see the older lady named Judy. One man thanked her for being his Sunday school teacher. A woman thanked her for being kind to her in the cafeteria at school. Next, a gentleman thanked her for helping him find his mother in a grocery store when he got lost as a child. A couple of people thanked her for making crocheted afghans for them. A man thanked her for giving him his first job mowing yards. A lady hugged her neck and thanked her for listening when she needed a friend. A couple told her how much her service at the homeless shelter meant to them because they were able to eat and have a place to stay.

Lastly, a lady came up and thanked her. She told her that she had prayed to God after her husband left her, but that she wasn't getting the answers she needed. She had felt alone and defeated. One day, she decided life wasn't worth living anymore. She was planning to end it all because she thought no one cared. But she found a card in her mailbox from this sweet lady. The card had a kind note and scripture that said, "My dear, if you ever need a friend, I am here for you as a sister in Christ. Remember that this is only one page in your book. God isn't finished writing your story. 'For we know that God works ALL things together for the good of those who love Him, who are called according to His purpose.' —Romans 8:28 (BSB). God bless you, Judy."

Because of that card, this woman had decided that she wasn't alone, that God hadn't forgotten her, and that He did have a plan for her future. Judy had saved someone's life simply by being obedient to God and following the prompting of the Holy Spirit. She felt led to send her fellow church member a card of encouragement, and in doing so, God had blessed this lady in more ways than Judy could ever imagine.

"See, Lizzie? There's a lot more to life than we realize. Too often, we blow off the prompting of the Holy Spirit because we are worried about what others might think. We fear making a fool of ourselves or being embarrassed for being out of our comfort zones. All those feelings are exactly what Satan wants us to believe so that we won't follow through with God's prompting. Satan knows the lies that will prevent us from doing our part to further God's kingdom, so he throws every one of them at us that we might possibly believe, hoping one will stick," Donald said with a nudge.

"I think I'm beginning to see that." I nodded in agreement.

"There's one more thing I want you to see," Donald said, pointing at the screen again.

The window went to a scene that was like a beautiful sunset across the horizon of the ocean. The water was crystal clear, and there was a fog of fluffy clouds surrounding the scene like a photo frame. Flowers somehow bloomed in the brightest colors all along the bottom of the ocean. Instead of sand, there were the most beautiful blooms. They were the good-smelling kinds too! It reminded me of a flower shop that my friend's family had owned when I was a little kid.

There was a pathway of soft, lush green grass. Butterflies and birds flew all around. And over in the distance, I could see and hear the babbling of a tiny brook. It had a little waterfall that cascaded gently over the rocks into a pool of water behind a set of golden gates with pearl-like knobs at the top and on the lock. They sparkled and shined in the light of the sun's rays.

I saw a young boy, about sixteen or so, walking up the hill along the grassy pathway. He had a smile on his face, like he was excited to be heading that direction. As he got about halfway up the path, a floppy-eared dog came bouncing up the hill beside him.

"Bernie? Is that you?" the boy asked.

The dog jumped up, knocking him down. The boy hugged his dog, and they rolled together through the grass. Bernie licked him in the face, and the boy took both hands and shook the dog's ears from side to side.

"Donnie, that's … that's you," I shouted.

Together, Bernie and Donnie walked up the hill toward the gates. As they got closer, the gates opened slowly, and a man who appeared to be in his thirties walked around the corner and through them. He wore what looked like some sort of white- and light blue robe and a pair of sandals. He had olive skin, brown, wavy hair, and a short beard. His eyes were the most brilliant shade of blue I've ever seen.

As he came into view, Donnie ran to him like he'd known him his whole life. Bernie even ran to him! He stretched out his arms and welcomed Donnie and Bernie both. Donnie just fell into his arms with tears of joy. The man wiped the tears from Donnie's eyes and put his right arm around him.

"Welcome home, Donnie," the man said.

"Holy crap, Donnie! That's Jesus," I said in awe. "I

mean, there's probably no such thing as holy crap, but if there was, this is where it would be. I don't mean that in an irreverent way."

"Stop," Donald interrupted me.

"Okay," I said, still in shock at the wonderful sight I just saw.

The window then became foggy and slowly faded away. It was like a vapor floating away in the wind. We were now back to the beautiful mountains and horizon.

"Donnie, thank you. I needed to see all of this. I've been so wrapped up in how I felt. I've not been able to see past myself. Selfishly, all I've wanted was you back. I wanted things to be the way they were, the way I knew them best. I had no idea what I'd be keeping you from if I'd actually gotten my way."

Donald hugged me. We got up, got in the car, and headed back to town. He drove me home to our house. We sat down and ate supper with Nana. It was her specialty, fried-green tomatoes, green beans, corn on the cob, warm cornbread, and cucumber and onions fresh from the garden. It was a perfect southern summer supper followed by homemade ice cream for dessert.

We laughed, reminisced, teased, and talked for hours. In fact, Donnie and I sat up in the living room so late that we fell asleep on the couch and in the recliner just like when we were kids, refusing to be the first to go to sleep. I'm pretty sure I fell asleep talking because I don't remember ever stopping. My head just tipped over, midsentence, I do believe. Yeah, yesterday was a pretty cool day, but today? Today was priceless!

Chapter 14

CHRISTMAS DAY

*T*he next morning, we woke to a wonderful Christmas breakfast! Nana had prepared a feast. There were fresh-baked biscuits, gravy, bacon, sausage, fresh-picked fruits, eggs, pancakes, casseroles, and more! We had fresh-squeezed orange juice, grape juice, milk, and coffee. Amazingly, I was able to sample it all without feeling overstuffed.

"Nana, how in Heaven did you ever prepare such a spread by yourself? You must be exhausted," I exclaimed.

"Not at all. I love every minute of it and enjoy watching you all indulge even more," she replied.

"But how?"

"Oh, child, have you learned nothing during your stay here? All things are possible with God," she smiled.

"You're right, Nana. God is good!"

Donnie hopped up from the table. "Well, it's time for gifts."

"Oh, I'm sorry. I am afraid I wasn't really prepared for all of this," I blurted out to them both.

"We'll let you off the hook this time." Donnie grinned that sneaky grin.

"Come on. We've got something to show you!"

Nana, Donnie, and I all headed out the door to his car. He drove us down the road to the town where we had met at the diner. As we pulled into town, I couldn't believe my eyes! Everything was simply charming. It looked like a small town from a Hallmark Christmas movie. Each building was adorned with evergreens and ribbons. Lights were strung across the main street. People were out, walking and greeting one another. Everyone seemed dressed in their Christmas best. There was snow on the ground, but no one appeared to be cold. It was almost like a movie set.

As Donnie parked the car near the diner, I noticed that Dolly and the other folks from the diner were handing out hot cider, hot cocoa, and coffee to everyone who came by. You could smell the cider and coffee drifting in the air.

Carolers were nearby, singing the most beautiful rendition of "The First Noel" I have ever heard. I looked at Donnie and Nana as to question whether we could go listen, and they nodded and headed that way as if they had read my mind. It was just then that I noticed how Nana was walking as we headed toward them. She wasn't stooped over. She wasn't moving slowly. Her hands were steady, and her head was lifted high. How had I not noticed this before? It was as if she had stepped into the fountain of youth. She had to be over one hundred years old, but she sure didn't act that way. And really, she never did act her age, but here, it was a miracle.

The carolers were beautiful. Not a hair on their heads was out of place. Their voices were perfectly harmonized, and they sang with such heartfelt joy on their faces. They were dressed as if they had walked out of Charles Dickens's *A Christmas Carol*. Somehow, it didn't seem strange. It was perfect.

As we listened, I couldn't help but notice a tear welling up in my eye. I wasn't sad. I was simply overcome with joy. Here I stood with two of my most beloved family members, something I had dreamed of and only hoped for many times. I was surrounded by people with nothing but love and joy in their hearts. They were singing from the bottom of their hearts and were truly happy to do so. It was then that I felt an arm reach around me and squeeze my shoulders. The perfect brotherly side hug came just at the right time. I grinned up at him and wiped the tear from my eye. We laughed.

The scent of the freshly baked apple pie suddenly filled the air. I glanced over toward the diner, and Dolly gave me a wink. I grinned, and we headed over to the diner for some coffee and pie. We laughed and ate, enjoying every minute of it. After all, this was the only place I'd ever known where one could eat carbs of all kinds and never gain any weight!

"Let's go do a little shopping," Nana said.

"Oh, yes," I replied with excitement.

"All right, all right," Donnie said as if only to appease us.

"This must be Heaven," I said to them both.

"Why's that?" Nana said.

"Where else would my brother actually go shopping with me?"

We laughed and walked over to the downtown shops.

The first one we entered was a perfectly cozy little Christmas shop. If Santa Claus and Mrs. Claus had a cottage in Heaven, this would be it! I could smell evergreen, cinnamon, and peppermint swirling through the air as soon as we entered. It was not overbearing as some scents can be, but rather, it was inviting. There were perfectly shaped Christmas trees around the room. I believe there were blue spruce, white pine, balsam fir, and Douglas fir to name a few. They surrounded the perimeter of the cottage like shop in a circular shape. Each one was decorated uniquely with different types of ornaments.

There was a train tree. It had wooden trains, metal trains, copper trains, colorful trains, plush trains, and even some made of tiny Lego blocks! There were steam engines, passenger trains, streetcars, freight trains, subway trains, and even monorail ornaments. Some lit up with lights, some played music, and one even blew steam from its top. There was a special train that went around the bottom of the tree on its track and was the most realistic model of a train that I think I've ever seen. I couldn't help but think of my daddy when I saw it. He loved trains, and I would have loved for him to see this one. In my heart, I knew that one day he would.

As I walked around to the next tree, I noticed it was a dancer's tree. It was full of beautifully dressed dancers of all types: ballerinas, tap dancers, jazz dancers, modern dancers, contemporary dancers, liturgical dancers, acrobatics, and dancing angels. There was an ornament quoting Psalm 149:3 that read, "Praise His name with dancing" (Psalms 149:3a, NIV). I found it very special because I grew up dancing. It was one of my favorite hobbies. I grew up in a church that was different from some because, from time to time, they allowed us to perform liturgical dances to worship God. This verse is one I often reflected on as a youth when some of the older folks frowned upon this form of worship in the church house. I decided I might actually purchase the ornament, but then it occurred to me that I didn't have any money. I put my hands on the ornament and flipped it over to look for a price tag, just being curious. When I turned it around, I saw that it had a tiny gold sticker that said, "Made in Heaven." Below that, it said, "Free."

I couldn't believe my eyes. I quickly looked behind the other ornaments. Each one said the same thing. "Made in Heaven. Free." When I asked Nana and Donnie about it, they explained that it was simple: God is love. Everything in Heaven is God's creation and is made with love. Just like His love, His creation is freely given and available to all who seek it.

Amazed at the chance to have free souvenirs from Heaven, I wanted to look the whole shop over from top to bottom. I passed an angel tree with every sort of angel one could imagine. There was also a tree with miniature toys of every kind—toys that bounced, rolled, made music, lit up, and more! And then there was a snow tree with snowflake garland, perfectly hand-painted snow scenes on ornaments, and what appeared to be real snow that didn't melt off the branches! I couldn't believe my eyes. What had seemed impossible to me in the past was absolutely possible in Heaven.

After I had viewed the rest of the amazingly beautiful trees, I walked over to the most cozy and inviting fireplace, where stockings hung on the mantle. Mugs of hot cocoa and cookies sat on the table in front of the fire. There was a red, white, and green rug beneath the table, and a rocking chair sat next to it with a handmade Christmas quilt hung across the back. The quilt had gingerbread people sewn onto every square. In the center of the mantle was a tiny ceramic nativity scene.

Leaning in to get a closer look, I noticed something unique about the stockings. Each one had a name embroidered on it, and one of them had my name on it. I turned to tell Donnie, but before I even got the words out of my mouth, he grinned and nodded as if to say, "Yep, it's for you." I reached up, took my stocking, and sat down in the rocking chair. Just as I started to put my hand inside to see what was in there, Nana spoke up. "We will give you a few minutes to yourself," she said. And they stepped outside the shop.

I looked around and realized I was by myself. The store clerks were not even around. It seemed odd to me, but then again I remembered that nothing was as it seemed here. I sat back, reached into my stocking, and pulled out a tiny gold box. It was shiny and small enough to fit in the palm of my hand. I noticed a clasp on the front of the box where it could be opened, and naturally, I was curious to see what was inside. I lifted the lid and saw royal blue velvet on the inside. Something sitting on the velvet lit up and lifted into the air like a vapor when I opened the box. It floated up into the air before me and formed a screen of sorts, like for a miniature movie. The screen had what seemed to be a white scroll with golden letters that were handwritten before my eyes.

The first words I saw were, "Yet you do not know what your life will be like tomorrow. You are just a vapor that appears for a little while and then vanishes away" (James 4:14, NASB). This was so true and so appropriate for me to see. I began to ponder what it meant for me. My life was not my own. It was a gift from God above and meant to be treasured. He had planned for greater things than just my own selfish desires. My purpose was to love and be loved. Nothing in the life I lived on Earth could ever be as wonderful as the Heaven God offered. But it could be as full of love as I would allow.

Should I continue to hold on to unforgiveness and pout because things did not go my way? I could choose to focus on the hurt, sadness, frustration, and trouble, as the enemy hoped I would. Or I could choose to fill every moment with the promise of hope and love that I knew God had waiting for me. If I chose not to, how would the rest of the world ever know of His love? If I was not loving, how would anyone know? How would they know if I did not have love in my own heart? How would they know if I didn't share?

No, it wasn't all up to me. God didn't put such pressure on my shoulders. However, He did put the very people I need around me. He placed those who needed me by my side at exactly the moment intended. If I was too busy looking inwardly at myself, I wouldn't notice the child I could give confidence to by helping him or her to learn something new. I'd miss the chance to hold the door for and smile at the elderly gentleman who thinks no one sees him anymore. I'd fail to see the clerk at the grocery counter whose heart is broken and who needs someone to give her a laugh and smile at the very moment I pass through her line. It wasn't all up to me, but it was up to me to make the most of what I'd been given.

I had a true realization of the gift I was given by God. I knew at that moment exactly what I needed to do. I knelt down right there on the rug of the Christmas shop. In front of the warm and cozy fireplace, I began to pray. "Father God, thank you! Thank you for another chance. Thank you for not giving up on me. Forgive me. I've been wrong. I've been selfish. I allowed my hurt to hurt those around me. I've let my misunderstanding and heartache get the best of me and turn it to the worst of me."

Tears began to roll down my cheeks. "I'm sorry. I have been given many people to love—so many chances to love and be loved. I've failed to see that everyone hurts. Everybody has their own struggles and pain, not just me. I've also failed to remember that life on earth is not the end. It's just the beginning. It's a chance to give others the gift of your love and to know your peace. Help me to look up, Father, to look around and see where I am needed most during the time you have given me.

"And most importantly, thank you for your salvation. You sent the only son you had, from this place that knows no heartache, to the place where He experienced the ultimate heartache. You did that for me and anyone else who would accept such a sacrifice. Your grace is so undeserved but so very much appreciated. Thank you for this visit here to see my brother! I know I don't deserve it. I don't know why you're so patient and good to me, but I won't waste a moment of the life you've given me anymore. I will be better for you. I will do better for you. I am changed forever. I am changed because of you."

When I looked up from my prayer, I noticed a box of tissues sitting on the table in front of me. I hadn't noticed it before, but there it was. I smiled and chuckled to myself as I wiped my eyes and nose. I took a deep breath, stood up, and glanced around the little Christmas shop once more to pull myself together again. Just then, the shop door opened, and Christmas bells rang to the tune of "Silent Night." Funny … I didn't even notice that when we came in the door. It was Donnie.

"Momma is sure gonna love this place when she gets here. She loves all things Christmas, you know," I told him.

"She sure will," he replied with that special grin.

I grinned back. "I think I know what else she'll love."

He gave me a big, firm big brother hug. I held tight, knowing in my heart that it wouldn't be the last. "Come on," he said. "We've got something to show ya."

"More?"

"Yep." He opened the door, and we headed out to join Nana.

Chapter 15

THE LORD HAS COME

Nana, Donnie, and I walked together down the block and over to the town square. There, in the center of the town, everyone was gathered for a Christmas celebration. Everyone surrounded the largest, most beautiful evergreen Christmas tree I've ever seen in all my life. In front of the tree sat an orchestra with instruments of every kind. The musicians were wearing handsome green suits and pretty red dresses. They began to play the most magical music my ears have ever heard.

"Joy to the world, the Lord is come. Let earth receive her King!" I heard a choir sing, and the people around me began to join in the singing as well. I had been so busy looking around me that I forgot to look up at the tree. When I did, I noticed that the ornaments of the tree were alive! Each "ornament" was actually a person wearing a bright, solid-colored satin cape that was draped around each one like a choir robe. Before each person's face was a light that shone to highlight him or her as the choir sang. Above each head,

I noticed something else that glowed: a bright light in the shape of a circle. You might say they were angels with halos. I don't know if that's so, but they glowed like I thought angels would. And they sang like no one I've ever heard.

There were poinsettias of red and white along each row of greenery where the vocalists stood. Red-and-white-striped ribbon was draped from bloom to bloom. Somehow, the smile of each singer twinkled, just as the greenery did with hints of snow on the ends of the branches. The bottom of the tree was surrounded with small children. They were gathered and dressed in what, on Earth, we would call their Sunday best. Each one sang right along with the choir. They smiled and belted out the chorus from the bottom of their little hearts.

As the song came to an end, everyone cheered and clapped. It was quite the celebration. Then, a gentleman wearing a bright-white robe walked up to the stage beneath the tree. He stepped up to the podium and began to speak, and this is what he said:

> And it came to pass in those days *that* a decree went out from Caesar Augustus that all the world should be registered. This census first took place while Quirinius was governing Syria. So all went to be registered, everyone to his own city.
>
> Joseph also went up from Galilee, out of the city of Nazareth, into Judea, to the city of David, which is called Bethlehem, because he was of the house and lineage

of David, to be registered with Mary, his betrothed wife, who was with child. So it was, that while they were there, the days were completed for her to be delivered. And she brought forth her firstborn Son, and wrapped Him in swaddling cloths, and laid Him in a manger, because there was no room for them in the inn.

Now there were in the same country shepherds living out in the fields, keeping watch over their flock by night. And behold, an angel of the Lord stood before them, and the glory of the Lord shone around them, and they were greatly afraid. Then the angel said to them, 'Do not be afraid, for behold, I bring you good tidings of great joy which will be to all people. For there is born to you this day in the city of David a Savior, who is Christ the Lord. And this *will be* the sign to you: You will find a Babe wrapped in swaddling cloths, lying in a manger.'

And suddenly there was with the angel a multitude of the Heavenly host praising God and saying: 'Glory to God in the highest, And on earth peace, goodwill toward men!'

So it was, when the angels had gone away from them into Heaven, that the shepherds said to one another, 'Let us now go to Bethlehem and see this thing that has come to pass, which the Lord has made known to us.' And they came with haste and found Mary and Joseph, and the Babe lying in a manger. Now when they had seen *Him,* they made widely known the saying which was told them concerning this Child. And all those who heard *it* marveled at those things which were told them by the shepherds. But Mary kept all these things and pondered *them* in her heart. Then the shepherds returned, glorifying and praising God for all the things that they had heard and seen, as it was told them." Luke 2:1–20 (NKJV)

The gentleman stepped aside, and the orchestra began to play the one and only "Hallelujah Chorus." Shortly after, the choir began to sing. "Hallelujah," they belted out for all to hear. Just then, a woman, a man, and a younger man walked out from around the tree. The woman held the hand of the younger man, and he stood between the two of them.

I found myself joining in with the singing too. I couldn't take my eyes off the three people who walked up to the podium. They had an aura about them that seemed to make them glow. I was busy wondering who they were when I realized they each looked familiar, though I had never truly seen them in my lifetime. That's when it occurred to me: they were Mary, Joseph, and Jesus himself.

We stood there celebrating the king of kings, and there He was in the flesh! Wait, no—in the spirit! He was alive and well, smiling, and had the softest, kindest eyes I've ever seen.

I have always felt the presence of the Holy Spirit when my church family sings the "Hallelujah Chorus" together with our church organ each Christmas. It is such a powerful hymn! However, in this case, I was not only feeling the presence; I was literally in His presence! I could not sing loudly enough to share the joy I felt in my heart. Bless the poor ears that were around me. But that was something special too: my voice carried beautifully in Heaven! "That most certainly never happened on Earth," I laughed and thought to myself.

I watched as the chorus continued to build. Jesus raised His hands above His head as if He was worshipping in church Himself, and said, "Amen." When He did, I couldn't help but noticed the scars on the palms of His hands. They were healed, but the scars were very visible. It occurred to me that even Jesus, the very son of God, knew pain. His nail-scarred hands were a reminder that no one, even Jesus, was exempt to the troubles of the world. Yet, there He stood, alive! Smiling! Happy! Jesus was raising His hands to love and worship the very Father who allowed Him to experience all the pain a world could offer.

As the song neared its end, Mary reached over and hugged her son's arm. She grabbed His hand and held it. I could see the joy in her eyes and a tear rolling down her cheek. Jesus turned and offered His other hand to His earthly father, Joseph.

I leaned over to whisper in Donnie's ear. "What a joy it must be for Mary and Joseph to be with their son again," I said. He smiled at me, and I knew that we were thinking the same thing. What a joy it will be when our parents get to see Donnie again. What a reunion and a wonderful day that will be!

As we all sang the last "Hallelujah," the clouds above us began to part. Rays of light shone down over the magnificent tree. A light that sparkled like nothing I've never seen before came down on everyone and everything. Much like a rainbow, it wasn't overbearing. The light of love lifted the eyes of everyone there. It enveloped us all. I felt wrapped in love like never before. I felt as if I were a child sitting on my Heavenly Father's knee, leaning into His arms for hug and to be held. Peace overflowed throughout my being. If people thought seeing was believing, then they clearly had never felt the love of God directly on their souls like I did at this very moment.

The celebration soon ended, and everyone was able to greet Jesus, Mary, and Joseph. It reminded me of what it might be like to meet the president of the United States. They made their way through the crowd, and everyone waited patiently and excitedly. When my turn came, I was prepared to say, "It's an honor, sir. My name is—"

But before I could get the words off my lips, Jesus took my hands in His and said, "Lizbeth, I am so happy to see you. I love you. I will see you again soon."

For once in my life, I was speechless. All I could do was throw my arms around Him. He held me there in a hug. He didn't rush me. He didn't say He had to go. No one pushed or moved us along. I just stood there, being held in the arms of Jesus. As I did, it was as if I released or unloaded, and I melted into the arms of my Heavenly Father. Tears came, happy tears. They were tears of renewal and rebirth. They washed away my sin, my grief, my unforgiveness, and my frustration. I felt new, and I felt like myself again all in one moment. As we unwrapped from one another's arms, Jesus took my hands. He squeezed them once more and looked me in the eyes. Let me tell you, when you're looking into the eyes of Jesus, you see nothing but love. Nothing else matters. I proudly proclaimed right there and then, "God is so good!"

When everyone had finished their greetings and fellowship, Nana, Donnie, and I headed back to the house. We laughed. We talked. We shared blessing upon blessing with each other. I told them of my experience in the Christmas shop, and they weren't surprised. They were appreciative and grateful. They were praising the Lord, but they knew I was there for a reason. They knew long before I did.

We had shared a wonderful and long, busy-but-wonderful Christmas Day. Never had I known such joy and wonder. We held hands and said our night prayers together like we had when Donnie and I were kids. We prayed to God in thanks for the many blessings we'd received. Afterward, we hugged and kissed one another good night. We said our "sleep tights." I lay my head down on my pillow, snuggled under the blankets, and slept better than I ever had.

Chapter 16

THE NEXT CHAPTER

When I woke up, I had a tiny puddle of drool on my pillow. I totally expected to hear, "Eww! Gross!" from my brother, like I did when we were kids. I rubbed my eyes, wiped off my lip and chin, and pushed myself up from the bed. As I sat there looking around with excitement, I realized I was in my own bed again and at my own home. I was no longer at Mom and Dad's old house. I didn't smell a big, fancy breakfast. I was in my bed, with my sleep mask halfway on my head, and I had some really crazy morning breath.

I looked around at my home and then at the alarm clock on my nightstand. It read 7:03 a.m. A picture of my brother sat next to it, and I picked it up and smiled. It must have been a dream, but, man, it was a good one. It sure seemed real to me. I wasn't even that disappointed to find I wasn't still with him. It occurred to me that the time I'd had with him was a gift. He was more than okay now, and I still had plenty of life to live—and people to love.

I set Donnie's picture on the nightstand again, and the next thing I did was kneel down beside my bed. I folded my hands and began to pray. "Father, thank you. Thank you for this most wonderful experience. I surrender. I've held on to my feelings for long enough. I've let them affect my family, my relationships, and my relationship with you. If Jesus could kneel and surrender His life to your will, then I can surrender my feelings to you. He trusted you, and so can I. Bitterness, unforgiveness, and fear are not of you. The enemy would love nothing more than for me to believe it comes from you, but, Father, I know better. I've seen. I've tasted. I know what good you have in store for me. So, Heavenly Father, I surrender my all to you. Take my life and make it what you will. I am ready for the next chapter in my life."

I jumped up and brushed my teeth, got my shower, and wrapped a few last-minute gifts for the family. I gathered everything up and loaded it in the car. I wanted to make the day as perfect as I could. It was time for me to start making a change. I no longer intended to mope around feeling sorry for myself. I wanted to be the person who Donnie knew I could be. I wanted to be the person my mom and dad needed me to be. I still had a sister, nieces, and nephews who needed me. There were still many things I had left to do, and I intended to do better from this moment forward.

I even made some blueberry muffins before I left. They were muffins from a muffin mix that stuck to the pan a little bit and were a little burned on the edges—but, hey, I gave it my best shot! I loaded the muffins into the car and grabbed my coat and keys. I was on my way to a wonderful Christmas celebration with my family.

As soon as I got to Mom and Dad's, I gathered all I

could in my arms and rang the doorbell. I was a little early, but that was okay. It would give me time to tell Mom and Dad about my dream. They were a little shocked to see me and seemed surprised to see me in such a good mood.

"You're early," Mom said, hugging me as I walked inside the house.

"I know. I've got to tell you something," I said as I set the packages down inside the door.

"Are you pregnant," Dad asked. He had shaving cream on his chin. He was in the middle of shaving when I arrived.

"No, Daddy. Seriously!" I exclaimed.

"Is somebody else pregnant?" he asked, aggravating me.

"No, Daddy!" I smirked at him.

"I didn't make anything for breakfast. I didn't think I'd see you until around eleven thirty or so." Mom was obviously worried about not having food for me to eat.

"I know, Momma. I decided to surprise you. I'll tell you all about it when I get the rest of the gifts and the muffins I made," I noted.

"You made muffins?" Mom asked.

"Yes, I did. I'll be right back with them. Then I'll tell you all about my dream," I said. I headed out the door to my car. It was the best dream ever. It didn't feel like a dream; it felt as real as anything ever could be. Either way, I wouldn't and couldn't complain. I was so touched by the experience.

I got the last shopping bag of gifts out of the back and then reached inside the front passenger seat to get the basket that held the muffins and the dessert I'd made for lunch later. When I picked it up, I almost fell over right there. There, in my passenger seat, was a little brown shopping bag and Donnie's keychain from his car—the rabbit's foot that my uncle had given him many years ago.

I picked up the shopping bag and looked inside. Something was wrapped in tissue paper. I pulled it out and unwrapped it to find a small ornament. It was the dancing ornament I was given freely in the heavenly Christmas shop. "Praise His name with dancing," it read. I smiled and felt tears of joy well up in my eyes. I couldn't believe it. Maybe it hadn't been a dream after all.

I tucked the ornament back inside the bag and decided to take it inside to show Mom and Dad. I squeezed the soft fur of the rabbit's foot in my hand, put it in my coat pocket, and looked up to Heaven, thanking God. Then I headed back into Mom and Dad's house, ready to share the good news. God is good! Perhaps some dreams do come true!

Special Thanks

To my hubby, Aaron, for encouraging me to pursue my dream of writing and publishing a book. Thank you for always supporting me and my dreams. Thank you for believing in me and helping me to make this happen.

To my friend Annette Estrada, for encouraging me to take the steps toward publishing and for being one of the special people willing to read my story. Thank you for your motivation.

To my parents, thank you for raising me with Christian values that gave me a strong foundation for this life. Thank you for showing me firsthand how to keep the faith despite the storms we face in life.

CPSIA information can be obtained
at www.ICGtesting.com
Printed in the USA
LVHW090526140821
695189LV00001B/5

9 781489 736611